Dancing Daphne

and the Newfie four

Caroline Mannion-Butler

Illustrated by Claire Wilcox

Published by Honeybee Books
www.honeybeebooks.co.uk

Printed in the UK using paper from sustainable sources

ISBN: 978-1-913675-18-9

*To Boy, Boris, Rosie and Bonnie who have been the inspiration
behind the story and have always, been ready and waiting to give their
endless unconditional love.*

A House is never Lonely where a Loving Newfoundland waits.

Caroline Mannion-Butler grew up in Leicestershire, and has a love for animals and the outdoor life. She now resides in a small Hamlet in Devon and has the Company of her husband, mother and four very hairy Newfoundland dogs, Rosie, Bonnie, Boy and Boris.

Working full-time to keep her ever growing family in the comfort they deserve, Caroline enjoys a very busy home/working life.

Their Newfoundland dogs have been the inspiration behind this story and have given over the years an abundance of ideas to be able to write the book. Despite their antics, they are a joy to share your lives with and are very much, hugely important members of the family.

With special thanks to Claire Wilcox, whose illustrations have brought the characters to life.

Chapter 1

THE ARRIVAL

As Daphne lay on the grass, she looked up at the sky. What a gorgeous day it is today she thought. The sun shone down on her warming her whole body and the smell of newly mowed hay drifted over, as the farmers were busy turning it ready for baling.

It was Sunday, a day which she particularly loved, as she was allowed some time off to do what she wanted to do on her own and could relax and have a well-earned break. It had been a really busy year with loads of visitors and tourists generally, but she did enjoy it even though sometimes her feet really ached from all of the different surfaces she had to walk on.

Daphne, you see, was a trekking pony and she was part of a small group of about 15 rare breeds who were put together to form the

Neddycott Trekking Centre. It was a charitable organisation that was run by her owner Monty McCauley, and she was very proud to be part of it. It was hard work, but it was the only way to keep the Trekking Centre open so it was worth her efforts. Some of the group were quite elderly now and didn't manage to do many trips, but she made up for that with her efforts.

She rolled over in the sun had a good stretch and got onto her feet. Daphne started to take a look around the field, the farmers had now left and it was lovely and quiet and the birds were busy looking around for some tasty treats from the hedgerow. Daphne walked over to the stainless steel water trough, she could see herself in the reflection of the trough quite easily. She took a drink and walked back, glancing at herself, Umm she thought not looking too bad, she had lost all of her excess weight through the summer months with all of the walking that she had done and for a Highland Pony, not particularly known for their petite qualities, she was looking good. Daphne had a strong thick neck, thick legs and a rather large bottom, what they would call a 'J Lo' in the pony world. She also had a very long tail and a gorgeous thick mane, which she had brushed frequently. Now that she had been resting, she felt that it was time to do some exercise, and as it was especially lovely weather – Daphne thought that she would attempt what she always attempted on these sunny days, a brisk pirouette, followed by an Arabesque, which was particularly tricky to do, as she had four feet and these particular steps were designed for those with two. So far, she had failed to successfully master it – still she thought – early days I'll keep practicing. It wouldn't be easy, she always knew that this was the case – as Daphne was not ideally suited for being a dancer, but none-the-less it was something that she had longed to do ever since she was a foal and her mum had told her that she was very special. She was determined to make her mum proud, she knew she could do it – it was just proving to be slightly harder than she thought.

Humming to the music she danced around the field, jumping about, imagining herself in front of all her admiring fans. She had a red feather in her forelock that stuck out and jumped so high she could nearly reach the clouds – or so she thought!. The birds watching didn't quite see the same picture – they stopped for a while to watch her but alas didn't think that she was improving that much and hurried on into the hedgerow very quickly – they knew what may happen otherwise, they were wise to it.

One of the blackbirds put out a quick 'watch out Daphne is practicing' alert and small birds made sure that they were out of the way. The rabbits ran down their holes and everyone else kept their distance, even the moles were ready – they had specially designed seats with seat belts on them in readiness for the shaking of the ground. They felt the earth thump as Daphne danced around the field. She started with the pirouette and quickly smashed into one of the hedgerows – the small birds quickly made a dash for it… bang as she hit the other side of the hedge, with their haste feathers were flying everywhere, as they quickly got out of the way. Daphne, however, felt that she was lighter than air and continued her dance. The passing fox saw the birds fly out of the hedge and feathers floating around, and wondered what was happening. He peered through the gap expecting to get a tasty treat for his lunch and realised that he had made a big mistake, bang went Daphne into the hedge, just at the point where he was looking through and the fox was shot into the air several feet high and landed on his bottom. He shouted in terror – and quickly ran off as quickly as he could go – it must have been some sort of monster that he had stumbled upon – not of course realising that it was Daphne – something slightly different to what he thought.

The birds, and particularly the rabbits, couldn't help but laugh out loud as they saw him run off with his tail between his legs. At least they were safe for another day they thought – well done Daphne!

Daphne pointed her toes, she was really enjoying herself now and working up to her finale, the Arabesque, "one, two, three on your leg, two hops back, turn and land on the other leg". Daphne toppled over with all legs splayed. She picked herself up – umm it didn't quite work out – she tried again and this time it was slightly better and at least she had managed to stand up and not fall over, so she was showing signs of improvement!. The remaining animals were not quite so convinced, but did at least acknowledge that she really was a trier.

Oh how she loved these days, after finishing her dance, she stopped, faced her imaginary fans and did the biggest curtsey. They, in appreciation, were throwing her bouquets of carrots and other tasty treats.

Daphne felt worn out after all of that exercise and thought about her second love – eating. The dancing had made her hungry and there was lots of lovely grass just waiting for her. Daphne walked over to a particularly nice part of the field where some tasty clover grew and put her head down and started to munch umm delicious she thought……

As she was eating – she glanced up as she heard the noise of her friends in the distance, a large clap, silence and a large characterful clap again – she then caught a glimpse of Fred and Gurtie, the pair of pigeons nicknamed the F&G Post Express. She could never quite understand why they made that noise with their wings – but whatever, she thought it was quite soothing to hear. She gave a neigh as they went on their way and Fred dipped his head to the side.

They were busy taking around messages to those animals who liked to keep in contact with their siblings and looked like they had quite a load on today as they went by carrying the red sacks. Fred's wings were going like the clappers and dipped down and back up – it must have been some weight….."Afternoon Daphne" he shouted…."lovely day today"……most days she caught sight of them and indeed she herself had used them on numerous occasions when her mum was still around. Watching them fly was an art itself, she smiled and carried on munching.

Feeling that the warmth of the sun was starting to cool, it wouldn't be too long before she had to go in for the night, Monty, her owner, tended to come down to the field about 5pm and time was marching on, she thought she had better hurry up whilst she had the chance.

After a half an hour or so, Daphne was disturbed from her eating when she heard a lot of commotion. There appeared to be a lot of dogs barking near the bottom of the field opposite her own. She wandered over to see what was happening, as there was a house over the other side of the road that she went by most days when on a trek and she had noticed that it was up for sale. The property, Cribhouse Meadows, had been empty for many years and Daphne wondered if there might be some new owners that had arrived. The previous owners had been lovely and had very often given them a treat as they went by, but the whole house and land were badly in need of work, as that was a long time ago.

Daphne was rather excited to see who it might be, it would be nice to see the house with some new owners, particularly if the treats started again!

The barking got much louder the nearer she got and she leaned over the gate, that was pretty overgrown, with hedgerow, to take a peak.

She was right – a removal van was parked outside the house and she noticed that there were four rather huge dogs in the paddock at the side. She couldn't believe her eyes they were as big, no bigger, she thought, than one of the Shetland ponies at the Centre. She had never seen anything so big. She also couldn't quite believe how noisier they were, in her mind they were far nosier than the farmers who had been turning the hay. What a racket she thought – they were running around the paddock barking their heads off and not at anything in particular.

After watching them for about 30 minutes or so she started to get bored and moved to another, quieter part of the field, hoping that the dogs would soon start to settle down – she didn't fancy listening to that noise on her days off!

Daphne carried on eating at the top end of the field and this masked the noise from the new neighbours, and as she had thought, it was not long before Monty was calling for her to go to the gate. She was happy to oblige on this occasion, as the dogs were still barking and it had given her a headache – she was glad to go in this particular day. Monty was taken aback – "didn't take much getting you in today Daphne, hope you are feeling ok". If only, he knew the reason why Daphne thought. Monty put her halter on and she followed him back into the yard.

Monty had been busy, her stable had been cleaned out with nice new bedding and she settled herself in. She particularly liked new straw and glanced at the full-to-brimming hay rack. He had also turned the radio on and it was playing some gentle music - What could be better she thought to herself? Monty came in with her tea and she could smell the sweet scent of sugar beet gently mixing with her food – you could see the gentle steam rising from the bucket as he placed it onto the floor. Daphne put her head down and started to eat the delicious meal she had been so looking forward to. When she had finished, she walked over to the hay rack, sniffed the hay and started to pull some of the sweeter bits out. Daphne didn't munch for long, as she felt exhausted from her day, so it was time to get some rest. She needed to be ready for the next day, as she would be back at work and had noticed that the board pinned to the stable had a number of rides booked in for the week. She walked over to the corner of the stable, lay down and snuggled in the newly laid straw – it was bliss. As she lay dozing, she thought about the dogs. Perhaps she would see them next week, she might even be able to say hello, perhaps by then they would be more used to the surroundings. She drifted into sleep and as Monty did his final check-ups that night – he could hear Daphne snoring and knew that all was well.

The next day, Daphne woke up, she stretched and got to her feet, another day and it was a busy one. She also had an opportunity to update her equine colleagues about the day before and she was excited that she had something new to talk about – the dogs and yes, not just an update on her dancing, which she knew they were getting very bored of hearing. It would be a welcome change for them all. Monty came around with some breakfast early that morning. He liked the ponies used on the trekking days, to have their breakfast early, as they would be out and working at 10.00am. So he generally came around at 6.00am to make sure that they had digested it well. He had found Daphne already up though and ready.

"Well….you must have had a good sleep Daphne – you were snoring well enough" and he laughed.

Daphne understood every word that he said and he was right, she had a really good sleep and she couldn't' wait to see the others. Monty came around at 9.00am and got her ready for visitors and by 10.00am she was out on a ride. She had a little girl on her back who was really light, so it would be a nice easy trek for her today. While walking she took the opportunity to talk to the others and tell them all about the previous day and the new neighbours that they had. It was good to have a bit of a catch up and gossip and the trek went very quickly indeed. It wasn't long before the whole trekking centre knew about the new people. It would make some entertaining conversations she was sure.

Chapter two

THE MEETING OF THE NEWFIES

It was actually a couple of weeks' before Daphne had a chance to introduce herself to the dogs. The Trekking Centre had been un-seasonally busy with holiday makers. She had walked by the property on most days, but the dogs had spent most of the time by the house, only occasionally getting up to chase a tractor or the milk lorry which they could see over the hedge, they were obviously not used to the Countryside.

She had noticed that there were already builders working at the house, several skips parked up and lots of activity. Once Daphne could go back into the field, she would be able to see a lot more but some recent rain had made the field quite soggy, so Monty didn't want her to churn it up. She was therefore only allowed in the top fields with her colleagues, which she never really enjoyed that much, as it meant that she couldn't do any dancing. It was at least some time to catch up with Humphrey who, like her, was a little on the large side and tended to tower over everyone. He came in at a staggering 17.2 hands high and 1,200kg, but it was to be expected, as Humphrey was a Percheron Horse and Monty had purposely purchased him to help around the Trekking Centre with pulling the carts and fetching the food for everyone; you could say the more strenuous tasks were his job. He was a true gentle giant and Daphne, especially liked Humphrey, as he had a funny sense of humour and always made her laugh. It took her a while to understand him though with being French accent meant that his his pronunciation was a little tricky.

After another couple of busy months went by and it was soon Sunday again, Daphne was delighted that the weather had dried up and Monty was taking her down to the bottom field. The local church were busy ringing their bells for morning prayer, but they didn't sound as good as normal, which was strange, Daphne couldn't quite understand what it sounded like, but it was not as pleasant as she had experienced before. She decided to walk across to see if the dogs were about and as she got nearer to the hedge, peered over – one of the dogs appeared to be conducting the others with a batten, keeping in time with the bells – the dogs were howling in time – well sort of! to the church bells ringing. She moved closer to see if she could hear anything else.

"Boy" – said the one conducting "you are supposed to be singing to a 4:4 timing and it's coming out too quick – you seem to be singing the notes in quavers and it should be semi quavers".

Boy hesitated – "well it's so complicated, quavers semi-quavers, crochets it's never ending"

"Come on" the large dog said – "it's all about practicing no-one said it was going to be easy!"

Daphne couldn't help but laugh and the noise distracted the dogs and they turned around to see what the noise was, Daphne gave an almighty sneeze which made them all jump back.

"Oh – bless me - sorry about that", she leant over closer to them, wow she thought umm these are big dogs……

The dogs were intrigued and walked over to be as close as they could to see Daphne. They all sat in a row, tilting their heads to one side – Daphne said – "Hello – have you settled in?" "My name is Daphne, are you liking it here?" There was silence, oh thought Daphne, perhaps they don't understand me then.

Then, the larger dog moved closer – 'Hello' he said in quite a deep voice, nice to meet you – let me introduce myself my name is Boris".

"Very nice to meet you Daphne, we have seen you walking by most days". "These are my siblings – this is Rosie and Bonnie my sisters and Boy is my brother".

Boy was even bigger than Boris if that was possible, Daphne thought. Rosie and Bonnie were much smaller, Rosie slightly more rounded but Boy and Boris looked more like Bears than they did dogs – All were black with Boris and Bonnie having a few small specks of white on the chest area. They were certainly made substantially. It made Daphne feel less like an outsider as most of her trekking friends were more petite than her apart from Humphrey. There was something about them, she didn't know quite what it was, but she immediately warmed to them.

Daphne inquisitively asked "why were you howling at the church bells?"

Boris replied "we were practicing our singing"!. The other's all nodded in agreement.

"Goodness" said Daphne – not wanting to upset them – but really thinking that it was the worst singing she had ever heard!...

Boris continued, "We have always wanted to sing as a group, but we don't seem to be able to harmonise too well. We thought that if we practiced when the bells rang, it wouldn't be too obvious if we were out of key".

Daphne had a job not to laugh, - "well" she said "what a great idea, I think it's marvellous that you are trying to do that, I can help with the rhythm but I'm no good at singing"

"I don't want to appear to be rude, but you are all rather big for a dog" Daphne said, "what sort of breed are you? I don't think I've seen another dog quite the same size as all of you, you are bigger than some of our smaller ponies here are you rare breeds?"

Boris laughed – "yes, most people are quite shocked when they see us – we are actually, Newfoundland dogs – we are renowned as good swimmers, although Rosie is frightened of swimming but Boy, Bonnie and myself love it. But I struggle with my back legs so don't have the strength to do it safely now".

"That's such a shame Boris, I would be so sad if I couldn't use my legs properly".

Boris said, "I've got used to it now, although I can't walk too far, which is why we decided to start the singing, as I can join in with that".

"What do you do then" said Rosie and Bonnie looking directly at Daphne. Daphne explained about her colleagues and the Trekking Centre and that it had been set up to keep rare breeds. Their owner Monty worked very hard in order to do this and took in paying visitors to help with the upkeep of the place. She then explained that dancing was her real love and how she really wanted to be famous and how her mum had always said that she was special. She told them that she had entered a talent competition for the next year, so she really needed plenty of practice.

They chatted for hours and had a lovely time talking about some of the things that they had done over the years. The dogs explained that their owners had more than they had bargained for when they took on their mum, a rescue Newfie – as she was expecting and no-one was aware, "That's why there are so many of us" said Boris, but sadly our mum recently died, before we moved. Daphne knew what it felt like to lose someone so special, she explained that she too had lost her beloved mum a couple of years ago, they all had a lot in common. Daphne really liked them and they liked her too.

Boy said – 'I've had a great idea, so why don't we help each other, you help us with the singing and we'll help you with your dancing to get you ready for your competition"

"Excellent idea" said Daphne – "you can be my backing singers!" Well hopefully they would improve she thought. Together, they started to hatch their plan - "We'll use Sunday as our practicing sessions and in the week you can practice your singing too". "Perhaps we will all be famous then" said Bonnie. They all laughed and laughed. "Some way to go I think" said Boris.

The dogs and Daphne became firm friends and shared as much time on Sundays as they could. Daphne spent the rest of the week working out singing styles, and planned exercises for them to practice. She was fortunate of being able to listen to the radio when in the stable at night and there had been some really good programmes on, particularly on Radio 4 which had been talking about how opera stars had started and what sort of exercises they had to do to improve their voices. In particular there was a good one about how to stand and breath correctly.

Each Sunday, Daphne introduced new ideas to them and as soon as she saw the dogs she raced over to them to greet them and swapped ideas. Daphne had worked out different exercises as they were all so different with their tones. "Rosie you have such a high voice, so I'm going to give you these exercises to do, which will lower the sharpness slightly" said Daphne and "Boris, you have such a deep voice, we will make your own more of the base beat. Rosie and Boy will be the harmonisation. She gave them separate things to practice. In a couple of weeks with doing these exercises we can then start to let you sing again and I think that will make such a difference".

The dogs had also been true to their word and had been working out all of Daphne's steps one by one and had cut out in card where her feet should be so that she could correctly land at the right place – it had improved her slightly, but Boris was a little worried that they wouldn't be able to improve it to the level that she wanted. "Daphne" he said – "we all feel you need to start to dance more naturally and we think the dancing that you are doing does not suit you as you think it does. Follow these steps that Boy has sorted for you and when you have mastered the steps we can put it to some music – we think that you will love it – but it will take some practicing".

Boy followed on by saying "I have noticed that your toes don't seem to be shaped how they should be, perhaps we should get you some new shoes, which might help"?

Daphne gasped "funny you should say that, but I've seen these most amazing tartan shoes in one of the shops that I go by....they are absolutely gorgeous" – they listened intently– "oh if only I could have some like that, I'm sure that it would help".

That night as Boy lay in front of the fire in the lounge – he wondered how they could get those shoes for their friend.....there must be a way of doing it he thought– he woke the other's up – I've got a plan!" they all looked half asleep – not another one they thought!"....

Chapter 3

BOY WORKS OUT A PLAN

It was early morning and the dogs had eaten their breakfast – they were early risers and lay out on the patio admiring the views. Although the mornings were cooler now, they didn't mind, they had good thick coats and there was still plenty to see.

As Boy watched a blackbird pecking at the grass he momentarily stopped and glanced at the others and said – "so I was thinking last night of a way of being able to make some money to buy those shoes for Daphne"

"We are all ears" said Boris

"Yes" said Bonnie "How"?

"Well, Rosie and I went for a walk the other day in the very bottom field and there looks like there is an old orchard and vegetable patch – that's not been used for years. I think we could easily grow some crops and start selling them on the road – you know like one of those honesty box things that we have commented on before"

"Oh yes"" said Rosie "I've noticed those before and no-one would see us".

"Umm the only thing" said Boris – "what about our owners seeing us"? Boy looked for a minute and said "I think we would be well away and they are busy in the house at the moment what do you think?" "We could get the seeds there are plenty in the old shed down there that haven't been used, we just need to do some work on the actual plot".

Rosie and Bonnie both looked at Boris – "that's no good though Boy, we can't expect Boris to walk all of that way".

"Well I've even thought of that" said Boy – "there is an old Trolley in the shed – Boris could sit on that and we can all pull him down - he can hold the spade and forks on at the same time".

It sounded like a great idea they all agreed, it was worth a try that's for sure.

"Do we know how much the shoes are?" said Boris?

"Can't say that she mentioned it" Rosie said – "but I could ask Fred and Gurtie to go and take a look so that we have an idea – they will know which shop it is – Daphne said they have been in the window for ages so they won't miss them. When I see them in the garden I'll have a word with them – they like Daphne!"

"It's going to take us a while to sort it all out" Boy said, "but we are heading into the winter, so we can plan this ready for the spring" "Daphne won't be able to come down to the field that often either as they generally have to keep them in which will be to our advantage".

"Let's keep it a secret from her and surprise her when we present her with those tartan shoes!"..

Luckily, Daphne was in the field on the Sunday and they all met up. They knew that their friend wouldn't be able to see them for a while, so they made sure that they all had enough homework to keep them busy until the Spring when they would all be brought together again. They said their goodbye's and as Daphne walked back up the field she could hear Monty calling her. She glanced back at her new friends, she knew that the weeks would now go very very slowly for Daphne, particularly as she couldn't catch up with her friends and she would miss them. She could see Boris wiping a tear – big softie she thought. Rosie shouted, "Don't forget to send us some notes to us through Fred and Gurtie"......she neighed and as the dogs looked at her galloping towards Monty, they waited for her to disappear through the gate and walked back to their own house.

The Newfie four would look forward to the updates, but knew that for them, it was going to be a very busy time as they had already started to plan the work ahead and the very next day the Newfie Team true to their word - got to work.

With the weather starting to get cold – it was just the right time to spend some time in the shed – and the first thing on the importance list was the trolley for Boris. It was essential that Boris should be able to go with them. Boy was quite handy with DIY tools and got to work. The Trolley wasn't in too bad a shape, the wheels and structure were in quite good condition, but he needed to line it with wood so that Boris's legs didn't fall through. He masterfully fitted hooks on the side of the trolley to house the forks, spades, clippers and hoes and Rosie and Bonnie lined the trolley so that it was comfortable for Boris with an old duvet and covered it with a good thick blanket. "I could almost sleep in that", said Boris when he looked over the masterpiece, it's a great work of art. There were pockets in all of the side panels so that the seed packets fitted in and other necessary equipment fitted onto the back section. To finish off there was a ramp, that pulled down to make it easier for Boris to walk up, with two strong halters, that both Rosie and Bonnie fitted into to pull the trolley. Boy had another rope at the back, to take the weight, so that it didn't go too fast down the hill. He was sure that coming up the hill would not be quite so easy, but they would meet that challenge when they needed to.

The trolley was now ready to go when the weather started to improve and they next would start to look at the sort of things that they could grow on the plot. They had many months of doing this and spent a long time lazing around the log burners looking at different websites searching for new ideas and help on how to nurture the site.

In between they were getting weekly updates from Daphne – she was well, but rather bored, she told them that she managed to have some exercise as Monty let her loose in the open ménage once a week. At least she was having some exercise they thought. They longed for the spring and the nice weather to come, then they could go for Phase 2 but, for now, they warmed their paws on the log burner and had some shut eye.

Spring soon came around the corner – it was March, cold, but just the time to start to prepare the ground – the newfies had decided to try and see what the plot was like so they all went down to the shed – and un-covered the trolley. It still looked good, they were now armed and ready. They pushed the trolley out of the shed for their first outing. Boy untied the rope with his teeth and pulled the ramp down for Boris. Boris put his right paw onto the ramp…put pressure on it – not too bad he thought and started to walk up, it actually was quite strong and he got onto the trolley and sat down. Boy pushed the ramp back up behind him. Bonnie and Rosie pulled hard on the halter, Boris held on to the side and the trolley was on the move. They started making their way down the hill to the field. It was a very exciting moment. Rosie and Bonnie found it quite easy going pulling Boris – but Boris was slightly unsure of it particularly not liking having no controls and it didn't even have any brakes. Boy knew that Boris was anxious, "don't fret Boris, I have the weight

– it won't go anywhere"…..umm Boris thought I've heard that one before – but felt that they had all worked really hard. What could go wrong – he could just jump out? He lay down and actually, started to feel quite comfortable with the ride.

It didn't take them too long to get down to the field, but on first impressions - it was going to be a massive undertaking, as the ground was pretty well overgrown.

Boy went over to the trolley and pulled off a fork, "let's see what its like" he said. He put the fork in the ground, it bounced off….wow it was like concrete he thought – this was not going to be as easy as they first thought.

"Let's take a look around" Boris said as he got out of the trolley – "look there are some lovely old apple trees over there"……

Rosie shouted – "there are some plum and pear trees too". Boy walked further on – "and here are some nut trees too – almonds and walnuts I think – quite well established, they just need some pruning, hopefully we may get something from them"…..

They were truly ecstatic, but still gazed looking at the plot with some hesitation as the grass had been allowed to grow and had not been attended for so long. Umm they thought…..this may take some time.

Bonnie jumped to her feet, "thinking practically, – let's start by making the plot into some smaller squares and then do one at a time – let's see how we get on."

The dogs started by looking into the hedgerow and found some good stakes. They started to plot out eight perfectly formed vegetable plots, and for some reason there always appeared to be an abundance of baling twine left in fields – they were glad of it now though! "There done", said Bonnie, the squares were actually quite big – so now all they had to do was to dig them! It sounded easy, but they had already wondered if it was a bit of a job too much. Determined to do something they got to work

They religiously worked on one square for the next couple of weeks spending as much time as they possibly could – but didn't seem to be making much headway – they came back every night exhausted.

After another long day - Rosie saw the magnitude of the job in hand and reluctantly said – "we'll never do this" and started to get upset. Boris consoled her, "we will just have to do smaller patches".

"Look" said Boris "we have to try harder – we want to help Daphne don't we?" – They all agreed, but they were incredibly tired and just wanted to have a long sleep.

Bonnie went back to the trolley and pulled out some biscuits – "come on" she said – "let's have a rest for a minute" and they all stopped, sat and looked at their work.

To their surprise, they then watched a mound of earth moving in front of them. They all looked at one another as it got bigger and bigger, then to their amazement, up and out of a hole came a very large and very flamboyant mole.

The mole looked at them, he was like velvet with a lovely long nosed face. He was dressed in bright orange velvet dungarees with a red chiffon scarf and a pair of white gloves. Rosie just couldn't believe her eyes – he must have been the most handsome mole she had ever seen, gloriously turned out and impeccably dressed. Actually she thought – he resembles me! She chuckled to herself underneath her breath.

"Are you the Newfie Four?" He said in his very posh accent.

"Why yes" said Rosie – transfixed with this new animal in front of her.

The mole went on to say, We were chatting to Fred and Gurtie from the Pigeon Express the other day and they were telling us of your plans to help Daphne – we would really like to help too if you will let us?"

"Any help would be greatly appreciated" said Boy as he looked down at his paws that were so sore from the digging.

"Great, if I can help I will"- I'm Tarquin by the way, we all love Daphne she has always looked after our friends in the bottom field, my friends and I want to help you - we can help you dig it"

Rosie somewhat intrigued, asked why he wore gloves and he explained that he enjoyed gardening but tended to get sore paws and this helped him enormously. Boy could definitely see the logic in this.

Tarquin looked at the dogs – "let me contact my friends - stand back from the plot." The Newfie Four didn't quite understand how a little thing like this thought he was going to help them. Tarquin put two fingers in his mouth and made an almighty whistle which made the dogs ears ring……they shook their heads….

To their utter amazement hundreds more moles came out of the small hole that Tarquin had appeared from, they were all dressed in brightly coloured dungarees of many different colours. Tarquin was clearly the leader – he shouted to them – "Right then gals/chaps" – we have to dig this land for these newfies here - who's up for helping Daphne". The moles all started cheering – "we are ready they chanted….let's do it" as they waited for further instructions. Tarquin moved onto Rosie's back and jumped onto her head – "if we all go in rows 200mm wide" – he pointed "you can start by cutting the grass off and taking that to the side, once we've done that you can then make a mole hill, that will break up the land so that these guys can do their work".

The moles jumped into the hole on by one and within minutes the newfies could see the moles at work. Large piles of grass were being moved to the side of the fields and then, with ease, mounds of earth started to surface in the squares and before long, all eight squares were broken up and ready for them to work on. It was an amazing thing to watch.

In between, the birds had started to clear the trees from the long grass – the pheasants pulled at the long bits and the rabbits came along after and cut the grass in two.

The moles lined up. Tarquin looked over the site. They had made a really good job, every inch had been accounted for and the dogs were so thankful, it had saved them so much time. "Well done everyone" - Tarquin said to them – "a most magnificent and brilliant job." He turned around to the dogs – "just call me when you need me again" he said – "we can do lots of things to help you" and within a few seconds they had all disappeared out of site.

They couldn't thank the moles enough Tarquin's head popped up from the hole, "any time you need me" said Tarquin, "just stamp the ground and one of us will hear you if you want anything" and then within minutes they had all disappeared.

Boy thanked all the other animals helping, "Well", said Boy – "that was easier than we thought". The next thing was to set out what they were going to grow.

They packed up their kit for the day and made their way back to the house – it was nearly time for tea and they didn't want anyone to catch them.

It was indeed getting harder to pull Boris on the way back as it was up a hill, but they all pushed and pulled and managed it. Boris managed to walk up the last bit, which Boy was pleased about as he was about on his knees and his tongue on the floor. They all needed a very good rest.

That night when the owners had gone to bed, Bonnie jumped up and pulled down the IPad – she was pretty good at IT and had looked up many things before, particularly with Boris having poorly legs. She had even sometimes left the particular site up so that the owners thought that they had come across it by chance. It worked, as several times they had purchased what it was that they wanted.

This time, she wanted to see what sort of things they could grow, more importantly, what prices they should look for when they came to hopefully sell the product. She gently used her right pad on her foot to look through the pages.

As Bonnie read through them, she told the others and they put down in order what they should grow in each of the eight squares that they had. All they needed now was to make sure that they could get the seeds. Rosie said "we have some of the seeds but not all – do you think Tarquin will be able to help us again"?

The very next day, they did exactly what Tarquin had said – they thumped the ground. Amazingly, within seconds, there was Tarquin "At Your Service", he said. "Brilliant" said Boris – "so we are looking for some seeds Tarquin" said Boy. "We have some of them but are missing these". Tarquin read the list "not a problem – when do you want them by, could take a few weeks".

Bonnie looked – "ideally we have to have them before the end of April, otherwise we will have missed the season". "OK" said Tarquin –"I'll see what I can do – leave it with me".

The Newfie Four had managed to keep the work secret from everyone, and they had also been consistent in practicing Daphne's instructions for their singing too. They even thought that they were getting slightly better - or so they thought!

They just didn't know what Daphne would think.

Chapter 4

GARDENING DELIGHTS

The Newfie Four had set five of the eight squares with all sorts of different vegetables such as lettuce, radish, spinach, kale, beetroot, chard, sweetcorn, garlic, peas, beans and some potatoes – they wanted lots of variety.

Boris and Boy had set about making an honesty stall through the winter, so that they could sell their items – it was surprising what they could find from what the builders and owners had thrown out – Rosie and Bonnie had even covered the roof with some material to make it look even more authentic. All they were waiting for now was Tarquin to come up with the seeds that Bonnie had asked for – they were more oriental, so probably wouldn't be too easy to find.

It was nearing the cut-off date and Bonnie had a back-up if Tarquin didn't managed to get the items. It was the last day of April and whilst the dogs were clearing out some weeds – Tarquin made an appearance.

"Afternoon my little workers" he said, "I have your products"….

he whistled and again all of his helpers appeared carrying the sacks of seeds. "Where do you want them Bonnie"? Tarquin said. Bonnie pointed to the three free squares and off they all marched planting the seeds. They expertly covered over the seeds with their paws – and then without any fuss, disappeared.

Tarquin said "I have been true to my word and you are now growing Chinese Cabbage, Pak Choi, Amaranth, Oriental Greens, Chop Suey and Burdock. We even have Water Pepper and Water Spinach that we can cultivate in the river"

"Wow", you have surpassed yourself" said Bonnie, "We can't thank you enough", said Boy.

"No problems – always ready to help". "We'll try and help with the weeding too"…and off Tarquin went.

For the next few weeks the dogs worked and worked to make sure that the crops grew well. They got the water out of the River to water the crop, and they even started to clear up the orchard as the trees were bursting into bud.

Rosie and Bonnie had put some wild flower seeds in that they found, this too would bring in some much needed funds for those shoes for Daphne.

Fred and Gurtie had told Boris that one pair of shoes were £110 and they needed two pairs so they were going to have to sell some produce to raise the funds. He was not too sure how he would get them to fit though, but there would be a way, and if it meant that their best friend would be happy and able to dance in the competition – they would do whatever it took.

Daphne had now started to come down to the lower field and had noticed the vegetable plots Boy replied and said "oh yes the owners have been very busy Daphne" and brushed it off as a casual remark.

The owners were talking about it the other night too as Monty had told them what a good job they were doing on the vegetable plot –

luckily, for the Newfie Four their owners had just thought Monty had got the wrong house and ignored what he said.

"It's getting a bit close now", it will be good when we can start to sell the things otherwise we are in danger of someone finding out and all that time and effort wasted". They all agreed.

By the time that the Newfie Four had been working on the plot they had found some good friends, from moles doing the weeding to the rabbits controlling the grass around the trees, even the pigeons were helping by bringing in some water. The bees visited from the nearby orchards and everything was in full bloom.

They all stopped looked at the plot and they all felt delighted to be part of the hard work.

It was soon time to start to sell the items and they were all going to help. Another plan was ready to be hatched out.

Chapter 5

THE BIG SELLING WEEKEND

The dogs were so excited that night they had little sleep and they knew that they needed to do a lot of work in preparation of the selling weekend. Once they had their breakfast they were out. It was a lovely day and the sun was already coming out – ideal for them. They all made their way to the sheds, pulled out the trolley, Boris took his place and made their way down to the field. They were delighted to see that Tarquin and his army of moles were already there picking the peas and putting them into bundles for sale.

Tarquin the mole looked like a conductor pointing and showing everyone what to do. "It's all going swimmingly"! He shouted to the Newfie Four. They were really lucky to have such a lot of friends helping. Tarquin had even managed to get Fred and Gurtie and their friends picking the apples and plums that were in abundance.

The red post sack had another use today, they expertly took the fruit off the stalk and it fell graciously into the sack that Fred was holding. Once they had about 6 or 7 of each variety it was put onto the assembly line where the moles were busy wrapping them up into parcels.

The smaller birds were picking the blackberries, red current, black currents and blueberries. Boris shouted, "Leave some for yourselves" – there will be plenty to go around!" they fluttered around in delight. Bonnie and Rosie picked some bunches of wild flowers and placed them ready to go onto the stall.

Boris and Boy were busy setting up the stall, it looked really good and Rosie and Bonnie started to place the items out for passing traffic to hopefully buy. Before long they had the first batch ready for sale.

Bonnie and Rosie had trimmed the stall with Ivy and other greenery from the hedgerow, they had also utilised some apples that didn't look good enough to eat, and delicately threaded some baling twine though them which made an apple bunting, it looked magnificent as the apples were of all different varieties and different colours. Now they were open for business. They had marked all of the produce at £1.00 to make it easier for the passers-by and it was also easy for them too.

The Newfie Four couldn't have been more proud of their friends and thankfully their help was invaluable to them – they still had a lot of produce to pick and it was already 9.00am, but they all took a couple of minutes to look at their achievements – it was truly remarkable.....

It was just after 9.30am and they could hear a van pull up – a slight man got out of the van and the other passenger who was much bigger wound his window down. "Eh look Bill – it's all labelled £1.00.

"Looks good stuff too" said Rob, the other man in the van –

"bet it's pragmatic" said Bill – "you mean organic" Rob said and laughed…."oh yeah" Bill said "that's it…anyway it would be expensive normally…..So who's going to know if we take a bit more than £1.00 worth" and laughed. With that they quickly got into the van and started to reverse closer to the produce.

Fred and Gurtie could see what was going on and put out a quick SOS to everyone, when Bill got out of the van and started to open up his doors – Fred and Gurtie's friends went into overdrive. They started to pick up whatever they could find and started to bomb them. Old cow pats, water collected from the river, old apples, plums, small potatoes, walnuts and almonds, bird poo flew onto their heads and splattered their van. They went into battle with amazing precision. Bill shouted at his co-driver, "Rob quick – I'm being bombed by mad pigeons get the van windows up".

Tarquin had also whistled his own troop into action and, tunnelling over, bit Bill on the toe which made him yell with pain. The other moles were making their way to attack and Bill could see them all from the corner of his eye.

In between times the dogs had realised what was going on and started to bark and growl,

"What's going on" said Rob "these animals must have rabies" and by now Bill and Rob were not going to stick around any time soon. "Quick let's get out of here, those dogs are going to eat us"…..they sped off up the road with the doors still open and the pigeons giving chase. The pigeons didn't take long to pass the vehicle and started to drop things onto their windscreen. They zig zagged up the winding lane and quickly back onto the main road.

The Newfie Four hurried up and put the goods back before anyone else stopped. "Phew" that was close" said Boris – "could have been a disaster" said Tarquin. Rosie could see the funny side and started to laugh – everyone else started to laugh too.

Never the less, hoping that this was a one off, a plan was put in place so that if anyone else should think of copying them they would be ready for them.

The stall looked fantastic again. They needed to sell everything they could; the animals carried on clearing the site of the produce and they waited for their first customers.

It was quiet and gone 10.00am and still no custom – "perhaps word has spread" about the evil bird attacking pigeons Tarquin said – "let's hope not said Bonnie".

Then, in an instant there were a half dozen or more people walking by – one by one they started to buy the produce. Each time there was no-one about they re-stocked and by 1.00 pm much of it had gone. There was a small lull in passing trade but then again in the afternoon, when the mothers were out collecting the children from school, more produce was sold. They had already managed to get £220 in change and the honesty stall was overflowing.

By 4.00pm another group of people had come and gone and by 4.30pm everything had sold out. They had done it another £50.00, far more than they had ever imagined, Daphne could have the shoes. They all gave themselves a rapturous round of applause.

There was much celebration that day, congratulating one another on such a great idea, and Boris gave a thank you speech to all of the other animals that had taken the time to help them all in their quest of buying Daphne the shoes that she so wanted.

Now all they needed to do was to find a way of buying them – not an easy thing to do if you are a dog!

Chapter 6

LET'S GET THE SHOES!

It was a couple of days after the big sale and the Newfies had a few days off as they were exhausted and Boris had been stiff by overdoing it.

Sunday came around and no sign of Daphne which was very strange, still they thought, it was probably because they had recently had rain and the field was still a bit wet. They were sorry that they didn't have any time with Daphne, but set about looking to see how they would be able to purchase the shoes that she wanted.

Boy as they all expected took charge and had a flip chart on the wall with post it notes and arrows showing his plan of how this was going to work.

There were new things for them to learn in order to ensure that they managed to get the shoes, going into a shop must be under disguise, how else would they be able to purchase the shoes.

The shop was about two miles away, too far for Boris to walk so he would have to stop at home.

Boy went back into his planning mode – the only way to get to buy the shoes was to look like a human. He devised that if he walked on his hind legs and Bonnie stood on his shoulders they would be nearly 6ft tall.

It needed some work and some practice as they would need to keep it up for at least 10 minutes and then how were they going to ask for the shoes? It was all going to be difficult and they needed some help from their friends.

Armed with a clean note pad and a pen, all of the newfies went down to the veg plot, it was time to get some help with the planning side they needed some inspiration and they knew who to get that from…..

Boris had to stop in the house, his legs were particularly stiff and they decided it best for him to rest up. He was not particularly happy about it and made quite a noise when they walked away from him, but – it was the best thing for him, although not what he wanted.

His owners could hear him shouting and went to see what was wrong. Boris stopped barking as he didn't want them to realise what the others were doing. "What's wrong with Boris"? – the owners said – "oh it must be because the others have gone down the field and left him – they do seem to be a bit obsessed with that Highland Pony Daphne don't they? It will be shame when she has to go somewhere else won't it? It will upset the dogs as they have spent so much time with her".

"Actually, I think they have calmed down since they have been with her. Still not a lot we can do is there as the stables are being run down. Poor old Monty, he's just not making enough money".

"It's good that Monty is going to honour the talent competition though – at least they can all have good memories to take with them to their new homes".

Boris couldn't believe what he was hearing. Daphne was to go away. He was distraught. Their best friend could be taken miles away. He would have to tell the others as soon as they came back, there must be something that they can do surely?. Boris was not going to let it happen, even if he had to sleep there and stop anyone from coming in his friend was going to stop.

He also knew immediately why Daphne had not been down to the field – she must know what's happening. He went into the paddock to see if he could get hold of Freddie and Gurtie from the F&G Post Express. He needed to send her a message to tell her that it would be alright – they would make sure that it was.

Back at the stables, the news had already been received a few days before. Daphne was distraught and the other's shell shocked.

Monty had been into see if she wanted to go to the field as it was a Sunday, but Daphne was just too depressed and lay in the corner of the stable. She had not eaten anything for a few days and didn't feel like anything at all.

Meanwhile, Boy, Rosie and Bonnie had arrived at the plot. Boy did two or three stamps on the ground and within minutes Tarquin arrived.

"Hello again", do you need some help then"? Boy explained that they were finding it difficult to come up with a decent plan in order to purchase the shoes. He explained that they had to look like they were a human, but how would they actually ask for the shoes? Tarquin thought, "umm a conundrum indeed. However, I think I know what will help; it will need some careful planning, but it could work. Rosie and Bonnie – you need to find some suitable clothing so that no one suspects. I have an Italian mynah bird friend Misha, who can talk, but it will take him a while to get the words right". "What size shoes do we need?" said Tarquin. Boy was not sure, but they would need some changes in any case, so the best thing would be to get size 8 which gave some spare capacity to fit around the heel for her".

"Ok – so if I get Misha to ask for two pairs of tartan shoes size 8 that's all we will need apart from yes and no. We will need to practice though, and how are you going to hand over the money"?

Bonnie had already thought about this and thought that a pair of gloves would just do fine over her paws. They would stuff the fingers with some straw to make them look a bit more realistic. She would also wear a large hat and chiffon scarf to hide her face.

Tarquin was going to contact Misha and the newfie's came back to update Boris on how they were getting on and the plan of action.

They arrived back at the house where Boris told them what the owners had said. They couldn't believe it – they must do something, but what? For a start, Daphne must be told, but where was she? She still hadn't been to the field. The only way was to get to her and warn them of what was happening.

They would try and visit her tomorrow before it was too late. Little did they know, that she was already aware.

Fred and Gurtie had caught up with Boris and visited Daphne, they could see already that she was getting very depressed and dropped a note to her from Boris. They watched Monty go into her but before that,

She picked the note up gently with her mouth and opened it up – it gave her some hope, but she didn't know what they could possibly do…….

She didn't eat anything that night and Monty was getting very worried about her.

"Cheer up Daphne" Monty said – "I'll make sure that you all go to lovely homes it won't be that bad".

Daphne couldn't even think of going anywhere else and just lay in the corner and put her head down.

Monty left hoping that she would start to eat and would have to call a vet in the morning to check her over if she didn't pick up.

The next day Boy, Bonnie and Rosie ran down to the vegetable plot and met up with Tarquin. He was true to his word and his friend Misha was sitting in the tree.

"Right" said Boy – "We firstly need to practice the walk – Bonnie climb on my shoulders", she jumped up and Boy took her weight. It was more like a circus act for a start off, as it took Boy a while to be able to walk in a straight line, it wasn't easy.

Misha shouted "you have to wiggle your bottom – if you are going to look like a woman, you can't walk like that".

Boy swayed his hips from side to side – Misha said – "not bad, but you'll need to improve".

Bonnie found it quite easy, but knew that it would be a difficult thing for them to pull off.

Misha said that he would go as close as he could into the shop. Hopefully, they could distract the shop attendants so that he could get inside, that way it would sound much better.

"What are you dressing up as"? Said Misha.

Bonnie replied, "We are dressing in a 1940's outfit, long trousers and a bright top, with a bright pink floppy hat and white chiffon scarf"!

"The top is quite bright – long sleeves to hide us both".

Misha thought – "well your movie star will have a deep voice, but I'll start to practice I think we might well get away with it. I've always loved the old Sophia Loren movies, I'll have a look and refresh my vocal chords".

The plan was coming together. Rosie and Bonnie got the clothes out of their owners wardrobe and started to make changes to them and also fitted the chiffon scarf to the hat so that there was no fear of it blowing away.

Fred and Gurtie had also caught up with them and told them they were worried about Daphne, she was depressed and had stopped eating.

Boris was beside himself – "we must see Daphne", but they had to get those shoes it was imperative that this plan worked.

Chapter 7

THE BIG PURCHASE

The plan had been finalised and Tarquin had come up trumps with Misha – Bonnie and Misha had mastered the timing of saying,

"We would like to buy two pairs of size 8 tartan shoes".

"Please could you wrap them they are a gift so I don't want to try them on"?

"Keep the change, they are lovely and "thank you they will be so pleased".

Both Bonnie and Rosie had sorted out the cloths that Boy and Bonnie would wear – what could go wrong!

In between, Boris was writing notes to Daphne to encourage her to stay focused on the talent competition, it was only a week away and it could change all of their lives.

F&G Pidgeon post were very busy going forwards and backwards.

It had given Daphne some hope and she had started to pick at her food. Monty was pleased that she had started to do this and was encouraged.

The day had arrived and the dogs were nervous, they had never done anything like this before and it would take nerves of steel and a lot of good luck to pull it off.

Boy and Rosie had a bundle of clothes each in their saddle back packs which Rosie expertly tied into position. They would change nearer to the shop. They could quite easily go through the fields to get to the shop without being seen by too many dog walkers and it was easy enough to hide out of the way. They had been practicing a lot so that Boy could hold Bonnie on his shoulders now with ease. They walked into the room and Boris and Rosie smiled – "good luck you two". Boris was stopping behind but Rosie would be going to help them get into character. They knew exactly what they were doing between Boy, Bonnie and Rosie, they each had the plan well practised.

Feeling rather pleased with themselves, Boy was the first to step out of the door but in his haste he tripped which resulted in him falling over with Bonnie falling on the floor in a heap. Boy howled in pain – Boris, Rosie and Bonnie rushed to his side – "I've twisted my back" – Boy howled – "hang on – just let me rest for a minute". He tried to get up but he just couldn't walk properly – just what they didn't want.

"What are we going to do?" Boy said as he pulled himself up flinching with pain he tried to stand again but couldn't – Boris piped up – "don't worry I'll take your place".

"Don't be daft Boris" – Boy said you'll never manage it with your legs –

"I'm going to dam well try" he said.

"Take off the back pack Boy we have no choice" and Boris put it on, Rosie again expertly tied it on. "Come on Bonnie," Boris shouted – "We'll try and get as close as we can and then you can jump up on me when we are nearer the shop"; what choice did they have? It wasn't ideal, but they couldn't see Boy getting any better soon.

They met Tarquin and Misha, who realised that there had been some unfortunate accident for Boris to have been there, but followed along with Bonnie carrying the clothing and Boris walking behind. Boy told him to take his time and Rosie just hoped that Boris would be ok.

They seemed to be walking for miles to get to the shop, but actually, it was nearer than they thought with going through the fields. Misha was really helpful as could see well in advance if anyone was about that they needed to hide from and Tarquin acted as a second pair of eyes, as he sat on Misha's back in the air. He felt a bit sick for a start but was a bit more used to it now. The weather that day was awfully wet and that was making it even more hard going for Boris. "do you think you are going to be ok Boris – let's have a break" said Bonnie. Rosie agreed and Misha who was carrying Tarquin on his back also agreed. "Ok" said Boris – but not long – we don't want to get there and they be closed otherwise it's a waste of time". Rosie was worried about the weather. It hadn't stopped raining all of the time that they were out and the ditches around the hedgerow were beginning to fill and spill over onto the road. She had seen it like this before and it could be quite dangerous. She said nothing but was really worried.

"Come on then" said Boris, that's enough, let's keep going. They walked facing the rain which was beating down on them but they turned the corner and could see the shops in the distance.

For June the weather had been really unseasonal and their choice of clothing probably wasn't as good as it should have been but it was just too late now.

"Ok" said Boris "we had better get into "costume. Rosie helped him with the trousers, tied them into position with some baling twine and Bonnie put on the blouse hat and scarf and Rosie pinned it into position. Bonnie put the money into the pocket of the blouse and put on her gloves.

"Jump up" said Boris. With ease Bonnie jumped onto his shoulder and Boris groaned as he lifted her up into position.

Rosie, Tarquin and Misha looked at the 6ft lady and actually, they didn't look too bad. The chiffon scarf had disguised the face and the hat came down hiding Bonnie's long nose. The rain had started to abate a little so they decided to make a run for it before the next shower descended on them – they could even see the sun trying to break through.

"Be careful Boris".....said Rosie. Boris started walking slowly making his way to the shop. Misha shouted "sway the hips", and Boris swayed them from side to side. Misha quickly flew ahead leaving Tarquin and Rosie behind who could just look on. It was an incredibly anxious time. Rosie and Tarquin couldn't do anything but just kept hoping that it would be ok and watched.

As they made their way to the shop there were quite a few people about. The weather had not deterred them from shopping. Bonnie whispered to Boris – we are getting some funny looks – Boris replied, just ignore them and focus on what we are doing.

Misha flew above – "you know what to do don't you Bonnie? I'll have to sneak in before you see if you can hold the door open for a while I can't be too far away from you." Boris groaned – "just get on with it Misha."

Off Tarquin went – and Boris and Bonnie came to the front door. It was slightly more difficult than they had anticipated as it was a door that had to be opened with a handle rather than automatic, "Umm Bonnie said – first problem then". Boris could only see very little – she pushed down on the handle pushed on the door and it opened – a bell rang to alert the owners and she could see Misha in the corner of her eye hopping in – so far so good.

The attendant came over – "Can I help you Madam?" – Misha shouted as Bonnie opened her mouth –

"We would like to buy two pairs of size 8 tartan shoes".

The shop attendant looked slightly bemused at this rather strange customer, but dutifully pulled out the shoes and said "would you like to try them on"? He asked.

Bonnie replied with the help of Misha…."Please could you wrap them they are a gift so I don't want to try them on".

The shop attendant said that he needed to check to make sure that he had two pairs of size eight and if she wanted to sit down there was an area to the back of the shop she could use.

Boris growled under his breath and Misha miraculously said –"Oh Excuse me".

In the back of the shop the attendant said to his colleague – "I've never seen anyone quite like the customer we have in the shop, quite the celebrity – I have no idea who she is, but she must be some sort of Italian superstar"! How wrong they were.

His colleague ran to the door and glanced at the lady dressed in the rather bright coloured outfit – "oh – I wonder who she is"?

Whilst she was watching the other attendant checked to make sure that the sizes were available.

It wasn't long before he came out with the shoes "if you need to change the shoes – please do not hesitate to come back, we will always change the size for you if they are wrong".

Bonnie had already got the money out to pay and handed it over to the attendant and Misha shouted.

"Keep the change, they are lovely" and "thank you they will be so pleased".

The attendant handed over the bag with the shoes inside. Bonnie held onto the bag tightly and they were just about to go out of the shop when the other shop attendant came over with a book.

"Excuse me" she said – "I saw you in the latest Glamour Magazine. You look lovelier in real life, could I trouble you to give me your autograph? I'd love to give it to my husband he's a great fan of yours".

Boris couldn't believe his ears. What was wrong with humans they were just so gullible? This was going to be interesting. She handed Bonnie the pen and she held it in her paw as best she could and made a scribble, bowed her head and turned to walk out of the door.

Bonnie looked back, Misha managed to hop under Boris's legs and Misha shouted "Thank you" and Bonnie closed the door behind her.

"Quick Boris let's get out of here" and together they made their way from the shop as soon as they could with their bag.

The shop attendant was really pleased with the autograph, but when she looked at the scribble, strangely it seemed to resemble a bone, but undeterred, she was happy with it.

They managed to get around the corner before Boris had to drop Bonnie to the floor. His legs were killing him and he was having a problem walking. Bonnie helped him out of the trousers and they all ran for cover in the fields. There was no time for congratulating themselves.

They just needed to get back – quickly as the weather had worsened and the roads were beginning to flood. Rosie and Tarquin could see them in the distance.

Bonnie had taken the clothes and bag with the shoes to leave Boris free but Boris was finding it really hard going.

"I don't think I can go any further" said Boris. "You will have to leave me here and go back".

"You must be joking" said Rosie "let's just have a rest".

Just as she said this an enormous tractor came towards them and they had to dive out of the way. Boris went one way and Rosie and Bonnie went the other. Boris had managed to go down into the ditch and couldn't get out – the others didn't have anything to pull him out with and the water was taking him down towards the River.

Bonnie started to panic – "what are we going to do – he will drown!" There was nothing Boris could do. He was swimming but was not strong enough to stop himself from going down. "Quick said Rosie – Misha – take Tarquin to Daphne – we need her help – NOW!"

Meanwhile Rosie and Bonnie tried to find some branches, Misha and Tarquin were off.

Chapter 8

BORIS IS IN DANGER

Misha had never flown so quickly, Tarquin had expertly managed to navigate him to the stables. Daphne was lying down feeling depressed when all of a sudden a mynah bird and mole landed in her stable making her jump – "quick said Tarquin" "Boris is in trouble – he is drowning – quick you need to do something".

Daphne jumped up, "what's going on" she said, "tell me." She couldn't understand. Misha was also talking in a strange accent. Tarquin took a deep breath explained what had happened and Daphne leapt into action.

"Stand back" she said turned around and with both legs expertly kicked the stable door down.

She looked at Tarquin and Misha. We need to get Humphrey. Get some rope and show me where he is, quickly, we have no time to lose". Daphne neighed loudly, Humphrey looked up from eating the grass in the field and he knew there was something wrong.

He ran away from the fence and then ran up to it as fast as he could and over the fence. He went heading for the stables where Daphne was.

"No time to explain she said, let's go" – "Humphrey grab the rope".....

Rosie and Bonnie in the meantime had tied together the skirt and jacket and Boris was grabbing onto it with his mouth but was getting very tired. He didn't know if he could hold on much longer. The weather was not abating and it was starting to get darker. "Keep holding on said" Rosie – "we have sent out for help".

Daphne galloped as quickly as she could the sparks were coming off her shoes as they ran down the lanes. Humphrey held the ropes around his neck and Misha and Tarquin were holding onto his mane. Daphne had explained to Humphrey what had happened as they galloped along. He knew the area well and said it would be touch and go, they wouldn't have much time. They had to jump over several flooded areas and gates. What Daphne didn't know though – was how much danger her friend was really in until Humphrey had explained to her about the area they were going. This made her run even faster.....

At last – she could see Rosie and Bonnie ahead "quick", she said. In mid-air, Humphrey passed Daphne the rope, "You take the rope and put it around Boris as best you can – I'll try and push him stop him from coming down any further. He is getting close to the edge of the River and we will never stop him with the way it's running down". Humphrey, positioned himself close to Boris and sat down. He started to push himself backwards moving closer to him. In the meantime, Daphne had started to put the rope around Boris. Boris was too shattered to do anything, he just couldn't help, but he was so relieved to see Daphne and she could tell.

"We'll get you out Boris, don't worry" said Daphne......

With the ropes now around Boris, Bonnie and Rosie had one side and Daphne had the other, they pulled as Humphrey started to lift Boris up at the back, gently pushing against him.

Boris could see them trying hard and managed to make a last attempt to help. "Boris – when I say jump, jump", Humphrey shouted and he turned around and pushed him up with his nose – "jump NOW!" He grunted as he pushed Boris up with his nose. With that, Boris pushed with all his might, they all pushed and pulled and at last he was out of the ditch.

They all lay there exhausted, but just so, so pleased that he was ok. The next thing was to get him home.

Daphne lay down. "Try and climb on my back". Boris pulled himself up. She looked at Rosie and Bonnie, also wet, cold and exhausted. "Come on" she said – "get onto Humphrey, we can take you back home". Bonnie and Rosie looked at one another, they didn't like the thought of getting on the back of a horse, but were just too exhausted not to if they wanted to get back. Humphrey got as low as he could and they pulled onto his mane and got up. He was remarkably more comfortable than they had ever thought.

"Let's get you all back home" said Humphrey. There was silence on the way back home, they didn't tell Daphne why they were out and she didn't ask – she just wanted to make sure that they were ok. It took them no time at all to get back as Daphne and Humphrey were so much quicker than they were on foot – she got them to the house and bent down. Rosie and Bonnie had already jumped off Humphrey and they helped Boris get down. Daphne whinnied at them all, and they gave Daphne and Humphrey the biggest kiss of all time.

The horses watched the dogs make their way into the house and watched the door close behind them. They knew that Boris would be ok now and they needed to get back to the stables before Monty caught them out.

Boy had sensed there was a problem, but looked slightly bemused from inside wondering what on earth had happened – but he would find out in due course.

As Boris crawled in – Boy looked at Bonnie and Rosie – so he said – "where are the shoes"? In a moment they all realised that no-one had picked up the bag….they couldn't believe it.

But almost immediately, there was a knock on the window. They could see Fred and Gurtie through the door window with the red bag. They opened the door to find the bag with the shoes in it – "thought you might like these said Fred!" –

"We saw you leave them when you were having a lift back, good job that we were posting in that area".

"Thank goodness" Boy said – and with that thanked them, looked around at the other three and said – "brilliant job – get some rest – phase three is about to start"….

Chapter 9

THE COMPETITION

It had been a couple of weeks since the incident and Daphne was slightly better. The newfies had been messaging her via the Pidgeon and Post and so she knew that they were ok.

It was the big competition the next day and she was very much looking forward to it as the newfies were being allowed to attend. Boris had told her to make sure that she knew her steps as they had a surprise for her, which she was intrigued to hear.

Monty still had the sale boards out but he had not really received that much interest, which the trekking ponies were very pleased about.

Every time someone did show some interest, they expertly managed to have a limp, or fall over or sneeze, which put any prospective buyers off.

The next day was soon upon them and Boris, Boy, Rosie and Bonnie were ready. Bonnie had been busy and had made them all tartan sashes to wear for the event, they hid them away from their owners.

"Come on you lot" shouted their owners, "get in the van – "we are going to see Daphne". They rushed over to the vehicle and couldn't get in quick enough.

Once in – off they went up to the stables. They pulled up and the van door opened they all fell out in a bundle – they were so excited that they were going to see Daphne. Their owners laughed as they picked themselves up. "Come on you lot, calm down for goodness sake" said the owners and they started to walk towards the stables.

"Just behave yourselves" said their owners again, and the four of them walked away just having a sniff and looking around.

When the owners walked off to talk to some people they quickly made their way over to Daphne.

Daphne whinnied, she was pleased to see them again and they all looked so well. They kissed her nose to say hello...

Daphne was seventh in the competition, she didn't know who she was up against, but she would give it her all, particularly as the dogs had worked so hard to get her prepared for it.

Boris had a bag with him. "Daphne – this is what we bought for you and this is what we were doing when you had to come and rescue you".

She looked down as he poured out the contents, she couldn't believe it, they had got the tartan shoes that she had so badly wanted. She gave them each a big hug and kiss – "what fabulous friends you all are" she said – and tears started to come down her cheeks.

"Don't make me start" said Boris and they all chuckled.

"Quick" Bonnie said – "put them on to make sure that we don't have to do any alterations before we start".

Daphne placed them on her feet and they were a perfect fit – she loved them. While Boris, Boy and Rosie were quickly telling her the story of how they got the shoes - Bonnie went back into the bag and pulled a tartan sash out. "This is to go around your neck" she said so Daphne leant down and she put it on. It looked great. "Finishing touches" Bonnie said and pulled out a velvet headband which had the red feather sewed into place. Daphne looked fantastic, they were now ready to face their audience.

Boy said – "listen we will meet you in the ring. We will be there for you just remember to do the steps that I told you to and it will all go really well".

Daphne composed herself, and waited for Monty to collect her. When Monty came to fetch her – he was pretty shocked to see the new outfit. "Wow Daphne you look great" – looks like one of the trekking centre helpers have gone overboard with your look". Daphne – just thought to herself, if only you knew. Monty and Daphne headed down to the ring, Monty told her to stand until it was her turn and tied her to the standing area. She had a good spot and could see the other competitors

Some of them are really good she thought – particularly the Irish tap dancer, the judges had given him a good score, but she remained hopeful. Monty glanced over at Daphne and smiled, it was nearly her turn and she was last. She wasn't sure if that was a good thing or not – but it was no good worrying about it now she thought.

Humphrey, and the others had started to move closer to the ring to watch as they knew what it meant to Daphne. She could also saw the flamboyant mole – that must be Tarquin and his helpers and Misha had arrived. Freddie and Gurtie were perched on the telephone line. The bell soon rang and it was time for her to take her place.

Boris walked over to Daphne – and untied the lead. He proudly walked in front of Daphne, dressed in his Scottish outfit made up of a tartan sash and carrying his bag pipes.

As they walked in the ring, the audience gasped, she looked round and Boy, Bonnie and Rosie walked into the ring with long swords in their mouths. They went to the middle of the ring and placed them down. They too had tartan sashes on and looked ready for business.

As they then walked to the side of the ring, Boris joined them, turned around to face Daphne and started to play the bag pipes. He nodded at Daphne and Boy shouted – "now dance".

Daphne started to dance the routine that the dogs had set out for her – she followed the steps that she had formed so well in her head, but found that instead of doing ballet steps she was now doing Scottish dancing, the music and singing coming from the dogs was fantastic. She jigged and turned, her legs went in and out of the swords, expertly positioned. Her bottom swayed.

The music and her new shoes made her feel lighter than air, she flew higher than ever she had before. The audience were clapping and jumping up and down to the music, and dancing together. Boris was amazing with his bag pipes and Bonnie, Boy and Rosie were all in time, singing in key and complementing what Daphne was doing.

She danced for her life – round and round she went, tapping and spinning, she had followed the pattern that Boy had done so well and now Daphne was heading for the finale where she did the highest jump and a spin. Her headband feather was flying all over the place and then the audience gasped, she went, high, high into the air - it felt like she was going 30 ft. up and the spin was magnificent.

She came down to the ground, it was a perfect routine and, the music stopped. There was a silence around the Trekking centre for a moment, then all of a sudden, everyone went mad – the audience cheered and cried with joy – it was an absolute success. Daphne could see Humphrey and her horsey friends cheering and hugging one another. The moles were doing some sort of Highland fling. Freddie and Gertie were hugging one another, they had done it – and it was even better than they had all planned.

The dogs walked over to Daphne they stood on their back legs and took a bow – Daphne also pointed her front leg and bowed. They walked out of the ring and waited behind the ropes, everyone was quiet as the results were being sorted......they waited, seemed ages, but only minutes then......the scores appeared, it was clear tens from all five judges. The crowd roared, patting the dogs and Daphne as they walked into the ring to receive their trophy.

The dog's owners were jumping up and down crying and Monty, Daphne noticed was also in tears.

The dog's and Daphne took their positions and along came the head judge.....who could hardly contain his joy. They all received a bright red sash with a massive red rosette showing and a highly polished trophy. Boris took the trophy from the judge and carried it around the arena to the claps and shouts of well-done from the crowd.

They all then walked out of the Arena, with their heads high.

Daphne and dogs found the rest of the day a bit of a whirl. Monty put the rosette on her stable door, he was so proud of her and she settled down for rest.

The dogs went home, their owners were full of conversation about how clever the dogs were. They were truly wonderful dogs normally, but this was amazing in every way.

That night they slept, snoring in front of the fire as they always did, as their owners continued to discuss what they were going to do.

The next day, the newfie owners said to the dogs – "come on then – let's go out". They were tired, but did as they were told. Boris looked at Boy – "could have done without going out today, I'm a bit stiff".

Once they were in the van – they were off. It wasn't long before Rosie shouted – "looks like we are going to Neddycott" she said excitedly.

Boris put his head out of the window – he could smell them from here – they must be going to see Daphne again. He recognises every twist and turn as they went through the skinny lanes. He started to howl, his owners told him to pipe down.....

When they arrived Monty was waiting for them. Their owners opened the door to let them out – and walked over to Monty where they shook hands.

The dogs watched them as they walked over to the sale boards and ripped them down, screwed up the paper and put it in the waste bin.

They couldn't quite understand what they were doing, but watched as Monty and their owners had some deep conversations. After waiting for about half an hour Monty looked at Boy.

"There - he said – "you can see Daphne as often as you want – your owners are buying into the trekking centre".

Boris howled in delight – "see" said his owner – "they know what we are saying," did Daphne know, Boris wondered......and started jumping up and down.

Off you go then said the owner's go and say hello to your Daphne – and they were off heading straight to the stable.....Daphne looked shocked to see them but they all nuzzled each other.

Monty and their owners watched them, they knew that they couldn't split them up, they obviously loved one another.

A few weeks on things had changed for the dogs and Daphne. They could visit her every day and their owners were busy helping Monty bring the stables back into good condition. The horses seemed to all be happier now, particularly knowing that they were safe together.

But, the best thing of all was – Daphne, Boris, Boy, Bonnie and Rosie could perform their dance every week. Since winning the competition, there had been such good publicity. They were in big demand and people came from miles away to see the Scottish dancing Highland and the newfie four.

Daphne didn't mind – it's what she always wanted and the newfies were glad to be a part of her life.

People were happy to give donations for the dancing and Monty and the newfie owners would never have to worry about the future of the trekking centre.

And so it was, their many friends like Tarquin and Misha, Humphrey and Freddie and Gurtie met up every day – there was plenty for them to do and they helped wherever they could and on the Saturday of the show – stood around the edge of the ring – watching Daphne, Boris, Boy, Bonnie and Rosie all doing their performance which seemed to just get better and better.

But for Daphne and the Newfie Four – life was good, they cherished each another and knew that they would be together for the rest of their lives – they had plenty to look forward to.

What a life it was………

BV - #0174 - 270921 - C59 - 210/148/4 - PB - 9781913675189 - Matt Lamination